More Than It Seems

Jimmy Jurrell High School Series –
Book One

Books by Linda Scott Enakevwe

The Adventures of Lily Sutton – Hidden Covers – Book 2

The Adventures of Lily Sutton – One Drunk in the Family is Enough – Book 3

Mirrors – The Adventures of Lily Sutton – Book 1 - eBook

A Handed Down Legacy – A Lesson From Beyond - eBook

More Than It Seems – Jimmy Jurrell High School Series – eBook

The Adventures of Lily Sutton – Hidden Covers – #2 eBook

The Adventures of Lily Sutton – One Drunk in the Family is Enough – #3 eBook

More than it Seems

Jimmy Jurrell High School Series

Book One

By

Linda Scott Enakevwe

The Enakevwe that loves God

Circle of Friends Publishing Company
Houston Texas

Copyright Page

Ethnic Books Publishing Company
A Division of Jimmy Jurrell
P. O. Box 710352
Houston, Texas 77271

To my children and grandchildren

for their continued love and support

MORE THAN IT SEEMS

CHAPTER 1

It was right after the first bell of the day, announcing first period. Many students stepped into the building at the same time, coming out of the fog. They moved down the hall slowly, already late, but they moved as though it were lunch time and not class time. Not even the mural-like photo of the school's namesake stopped them this morning. Usually, when students did not want to go to class, they stood in front of the larger-than-life photograph of Jimmy Jurrell like it was a fountain and they had a hand full of quarters.

Claudetta Rawlings walked faster than usual to class, but no joy or smile seemed to be anywhere on her face. She had forgotten to do her homework the night before, and she knew her teacher, Mrs. Arnold, was going to ask for the work as soon as she entered her classroom. She had stayed at work the night before until eleven o'clock, and it took her mom another hour to pick her up from her job. Even though Claudetta had turned seventeen a month earlier, she still did not drive or own a car. Most of the time she caught a ride to work with her boyfriend, Rex-Tar, but it was her mom who picked her up at night and her mom who took her to school in the mornings.

The drive time to and from school and work was what Claudetta's mother called the "conference ride." Those were the times Mazola Rawlings used to teach her daughter little lessons as well as time to find out what her daughter was doing in school each day. "Mrs. Many Questions" was the name that Claudetta called her mother to herself and to her friends.

This morning, as she pushed her way to Mrs. Arnold's class, Claudetta was not laughing, and she was not interested in answering any questions. No. All she wanted to do was to take a seat and be quiet enough to figure out all by herself what she actually wanted to do with her life. "Claudetta, do you have your homework?" Mrs. Arnold asked as soon as Claudetta took a seat.

"No, I don't," Claudetta said at the same time she rolled her eyes about.

"No, Ma 'am," Mrs. Arnold said.

"What?" Claudetta asked, then stopped.

The other students laughed, especially Alfredo who repeated Claudetta's word, "what," over and over, but he said it like a song.

"Uh. No, Ma 'am," Claudetta whispered.

Mrs. Arnold walked back to the board, and Claudetta put her hands up to her eyes and exhaled. She was always tired and sleepy these days, but she never got anything done. She had no homework, no real good tips from serving food at the restaurant, and no chores done at home. Lately, that was her daily life. She was not happy with herself. Even in the daytime, she felt she could get lost in her bedroom and never be found.   Less than a year to graduate from high school, and suddenly, she had failing grades in every class but journalism.

It wasn't that Claudetta was great in journalism, but at least she did not have to memorize anything or know any numbers. She was good with her hands, and her project was to paste up a magazine using things that she liked. She jumped with joy when the teacher told her that she did not have to interview a real person or write anything herself. In her mind, what could be so hard about that? It was the one class that she had that she didn't have to read a lot.

CHAPTER 2

Rex-Tar, named after both his parents, Rex Dunbar and Tara Dunbar, had his own problems at Jimmy Jurrell High School, but his love for Claudetta were not one of his problems. He, too, wanted to be done with school in May, but it was just September, and he could not survive without a job. Graduation in May would only be possible if he attended school and he did not fail any classes. His survival would only be possible if he kept a job.

At times, he worked into the wee hours of the morning. He made sure all the pots and pans and dishes were cleaned for the next day at Club Restaurant. Being a dishwasher was not a high-paying job by any means, but it paid for his school clothes, his simple lunch, and his senior fees. There was no way his single mom would be able to pay the rent and bills by herself. She had not been able to give him any money for his graduation cost.

It would be four months before he turned eighteen, and he knew he had to do something to hold his head up high as a man.

He really wanted to be a man, because his mom needed him to be a man.

His job was not much to others, but he could buy gas for his old friend, his eight year old Toyota Corolla. He made enough to take Claudetta to the movies, but he knew that his job helped his mom keep the lights on in the tiny apartment that the two of them shared.

Rex-Tar joked with his friends about work, and they teased him about being a dishwasher, but in his heart he was glad he had a job at all. He knew he needed to go to school every day, because even in class, he had to ask a lot of questions just to keep up his grades. Still, no job meant, no home. No school meant, no graduation.

Some days, his decisions gave him too much to think about: Go to school instead of going to work, and the lights would get cut off for more than a week. If the lights were cut off, it would cost extra fees and time to get them back on again. Rex-Tar fought with himself on trying to figure out what to do. On days like today, he was late, he missed first period, and now, he stood in front of old man Jimmy Jurrell himself and thought about what would Jimmy do? Jimmy had been a family man to the end.

CHAPTER 3

Jimmy Jurrell High School in Houston, Texas was a specialty high school and a bonding place for a lot of high school students who had more in common than they knew. It was like they were sisters and brothers on being homeless or near homeless, on the verge of dropping out, and on being behind in their school work with low grades or behind in their grade level. Jimmy Jurrell High or JJ High was known as the fixer-upper high school, where the students got serious about getting on track to graduate.

Right outside the main office was a huge photograph of Jimmy Jurrell that had been restored from its original state in 1918, the year before Jimmy Jurrell was murdered. Below the picture were two sentences: *Jimmy Jurrell was a son, a husband, and a father. He died protecting his mother.*

Many students stood in front of that picture at different times of the day. It was as though the students were having a moment of silence, alone, with themselves. On this morning, before going to class, stood Rex-Tar Dunbar looking up at the photo of Jimmy Jurrell without saying a word. Who would think that the image and life of a man born in 1898 would get a second look from a teenager in 2016?

Rex-Tar, again, looked at the sentences below the painting. Even he had visited that picture enough to have read the sentences to memory. He pulled out his phone and dialed quickly. Within seconds, he said, "Mom, I'll pick you up for the doctor at one o'clock." He paused, then, lied, "No. I won't be skipping. We have early dismissal today. I just forgot it earlier."

At least four of Claudetta's classes were with Rex-Tar, and the other two were with her friend Marisol. Claudetta had learned a long time ago to partner in every class with a friend, because there would be times when it would be hard to keep up alone. Anytime she missed a day from school or anytime she found herself day dreaming too long, she could always ask her friend for whatever information that she had missed. It was not the same in class with her boyfriend. Rex-Tar counted on her to have the notes and on her to know the information.

Yesterday, both of them had missed the last class of the day, World History. Today, neither of them had the work or even had a clue as to what was the missing work that they did not have. Second period now and Claudetta turned around in her chair once again to check the door and the classroom for Rex-Tar's presence. No Rex-Tar any place in the room. She looked at her watch and then rested her eyes on her math's "Do Now" without a clue as to how to start to answer the two math problems on the sheet.

At least Mr. Woodson allowed students to partner to work the problems. Still, how was that going to help her any when her partner had not shown up to class?

"You might as well come to our table, Claudetta. He ain't here," Marisol said. "It doesn't matter who's your partner; just finish the sheet."

Letting go her smile instantly, Claudetta turned to look at Marisol in defeat.

"I guess," she said, and she shook her head. She looked at Marisol's worksheet, then looked back at her own. "I don't even understand this," Claudetta said. "How do you write the problem?"

"You have to read it first," Marisol said. "How you set it up is what makes Mr. Woodson think you know the work. He's not going to read all of the answers, just a little of them. As Mr. Woodson walked around the classroom and stopped and looked at each group, the classroom door opened and stayed open while Rex-Tar came in and took a seat at the first table he reached from the door. Without saying a word, Rex-Tar looked around at everybody looking down at their "Do Nows. He stood up quickly and walked over to a small stack of papers on the FYI table and took one sheet. Instead of going back to his first seat, he walked across the room and took a seat next to Claudetta, across from Marisol.

"Where have you been?" Claudetta asked.

"Over slept; missed first period," Rex-Tar said.

"Shhh," Mr. Woodson said.

"Here, do mine," Claudetta said, as she pushed her paper to him. "We don't have much time."

Rex-Tar rubbed his eyes and face before he lowered his eyes onto Claudetta's paper. He moved his lips in silence as he read the math problem. Claudetta moved closer to him like she did in the movies. She rested her head on his shoulder as he had both arms on the table. When she saw Mr. Woodson move toward them, she lifted her head and pulled Rex-Tar's paper back to her as though it were hers. Mr. Woodson stopped and walked

to a different table.

"Ten minutes left, everybody," Mr. Woodson said. "Hurry."

CHAPTER 4

Claudetta stood in the hallway and waited on Rex-Tar who seemed to be taking a while talking to Mr. Woodson, still in the class. As soon as the bell had rung, Claudetta had walked out with her finished paper to give to Mr. Woodson while Rex-Tar sat at the table and finished his own paper.

Already at third period, Claudetta looked tired. She leaned on the wall behind the room door and leaned over to rest her back side on the wall as she looked to be touching her toes. She took a deep breath and let it out as though she were trying to recharge herself. Another day of classes and school-work and she could not keep up on her own. The thought of months of school ahead of her made her want to cry. Before she could finish one lesson assignment, another one was given and due.

She continued to hang behind the classroom door, waiting for Rex-Tar as though her very life depended on him. Their working together, playing together, and going to school together gave her a comfort that she did not know how to live without. Being with Rex-Tar took away a fear that she could not explain.

Claudetta hugged Rex-Tar as soon as he came out of the classroom. "Can we get a pizza for lunch?" she asked.

"Got to take Mom to the doctor," he said. "You know I have the car. I don't want her on the bus and she does not feel well."

"Oh. You just got here, and I found out we have a test in six period, Rex," Claudetta said, holding him even closer.

"I know, but I don't have the time. I didn't study for it, anyway. Worked late, remember. Got work tonight, and Mom at one o'clock today."

She stared at him in silence.

"Come on, Claudie, you know I'm hoping to get out in May, and you and I both know, half the time, I don't think that I'm gonna make it. I'm asking Mr. Pete for some more hours at work."

"You can't, Rex. When will you sleep? When will you get to school?"

"I need the money, Babe. I need it…for my mom. Trust me. It'll be okay."

Claudetta's eyes filled with tears. She straightened her posture for a moment, looking at him walk away alone. Marisol had already walked to the door of their next class. Claudetta looked at Rex walking away, then at Marisol standing at the classroom door on the opposite side of the hall. She ran toward Marisol but not before she turned toward Rex and yelled, "Wait, Rex; I'm going with you."

CHAPTER 5

The fog had lifted and the sky was a powder white from the many, fluffy clouds that covered it. Houston Texas in September was like no other place on Earth. The temperature was a blazing ninety degrees, like summer was still in effect. Everything about the day was too beautiful to be in school. Skipping was not an option, even though school seemed to be the last place Rex-Tar and Claudetta wanted to be.

Tara Dunbar, a petite woman in her thirties, set on a concrete bench at the street corner of Gessner Street and West Bellfort Street. Although, the sun was hot, she still rocked and shook as though she were freezing. It was already one-fifteen in the afternoon, and she was already late leaving for her doctor's appointment.

She looked left down West Bellfort toward Fondren Road, and then, she looked right down West Bellfort toward Beltway 8, but no signs of her son, Rex's, red Corolla. The wind blew a little, and she pulled her buttoned-down sweater closed on her chest, and she bent over her lap and rested her head on her purse. She had told Rex that she could take the bus, but he had insisted on picking her up, and now, he was late. *Maybe, I should call the doctor and tell him that I'm running late*, she thought. *Maybe the school didn't let him leave.*

Tara never reached for her phone in her purse. She simply hugged her purse tighter, like the kind of hug she needed. The pain that she had felt in her stomach for a while seemed to get worse when she worried or when she was in a hurry, which seemed to be all the time now. She closed her eyes as the silent tears ran down her face. It took all of her strength not to lie down on the bench and give in to the pain. Still, sitting on that bench, she willed herself to keep going for her son, her only child and only memory of her late husband, Rex Dunbar.

"I am stronger than this," she whispered to herself. "I am the mother. I am the mother. I am the mother. My son needs me. My son needs me. My son –"

"Beep." Rex blew the horn at the same time that he pulled up on the parking lot of the tire store where Tara sat at the bus stop. "Mom," he called. "Mom, Mom, let me help you," he said, then looked back at Claudetta before he got out of the car.

"Why didn't you wait for me at home, Mom? Told you I was coming."

"I wanted to make it easier on you. Tried to keep you from having to drive back to the complex," Tara said. "And I didn't know if the school would let you leave, Rex, Honey."

"Left right after second period, Mom. I made the ADA, that's all I needed. They will write me up for skipping, but at least I was present for the school's record. It is okay, Mom. I'm doing what I need to do."

Claudetta opened the door and got out of the front seat and opened the back door of the car and put her purse inside. She ran over to Rex and his mother and took Tara's right hand and helped Rex pull his mother to her feet and steady her before they moved to the car.

"I'm sorry," Tara continued to whisper to her son first and then to Claudetta.

"Shhh," Rex said. "I got you, Mom. I got you."

Tears filled Claudetta's eyes and she held onto Rex's mom's arm as she fought back the many questions that she had for Rex about his mother. No matter how she asked the questions in her mind, she knew it was not the right time or place to ask any of them out loud.

"I'm going to be late for the doctor, Rex," Tara said. "Maybe, we need to call him to let him know I'm still coming."

"What time is the appointment, Mrs. Dunbar?" asked Claudetta.

"Two o'clock," Tara said.

"We can make that, Mom. Don't worry. We got this. Let's just get you into the car."

CHAPTER 6

Mrs. Lester, one of the teachers at Jimmy Jurrell High, called her attendance roll for her fifth period class only to hear silence when she called Rex-Tar's name. She called it again, "Rex-Tar Dunbar."

"He is not here, Mrs. Lester," Carlos said.

"I know I saw him in the hallway earlier today," Mrs. Lester said.

"Yeah, he was here this morning, but he left right after second period. I have third period with him, and he didn't show," Carlos added.

"Okaay," Mrs. Lester said, before she picked up her pen and began writing.

Jimmy Jurrell High, or JJ High was a small, specialty high school that served the needs of students who needed small classrooms. There were no video conferencing classrooms there that held a hundred students at once. The average sized class at JJ High was nineteen, and that was called a "big" class by JJ High's standards.

The purpose of the small classes had been for students to have the kind of one-on-one training necessary to get ahead and to graduate. A small school with small classes meant every teacher knowing the names of every student. It meant if a student did not understand a lesson, then, the student could raise his hand in class and ask the teacher to reteach the lesson.

Students were given an exit ticket in every class where a student could write down whatever lesson that he needed the teacher to teach him one-on-one. The tickets helped the teacher know who needed to be retaught a specific lesson. That feature at JJ High was certainly a selling point for Rex-Tar Dunbar and

Claudetta Rawlings, because both of them missed a lot of school. They had four classes together where if they both missed, neither of them could actually help the other one.

Mrs. Garcia, the secretary of JJ High, printed the attendance sheet for the day and began highlighting every student's name who had been in school at second period and gone by fourth period or after lunch. She picked up her phone and dialed Mazola Rawlings, a.k.a. Mrs. Many Questions and told her that her daughter Claudetta had left school after second period. The secretary was still talking when Mrs. Rawlings yelled, "Say no more; I'm on it."

CHAPTER 7

Rex-Tar attended school only on Mondays and Wednesday after Mr. Pete increased his hours at work. It was not that the restaurant suddenly had more business, it was the fact that Rex-Tar told Mr. Pete exactly how ill his mother really was. Pete had wrapped his arms around Rex-Tar's neck and pulled him close upon hearing his fears about his mother's health.

The doctor had found bleeding ulcers in his mother's stomach so severe until she was lucky she could eat anything other than applesauce. "You need surgery, Mrs. Dunbar," were the first words the doctor had said after getting back test results on Rex-Tar's mother. Those words had only been said minutes before the thought of staying in school began to fade in the distance like a far-away memory to Rex-Tar. Even if he went to school, he knew the thought of his mother in pain would not allow him to do much good on his school work. He had asked

Claudetta to pick up his school work from his teachers, but school had no place in his head when his heart was full.

Crew members at the restaurant noticed Rex-Tar's presence more in the restaurant but said nothing. Rex-Tar noticed them looking at him. He noticed his mother gripping the back of a dining room chair in pain, but neither of them said anything to the other. Emotions welled within Rex-Tar, but words did not form. All he knew was he had to work more so his mother could work less.

The surgery was a few weeks away, and he had insisted his mother stay home from her maid's job and her fast food job. Even though she had worked for the burger house for over fifteen years, she still only made eight dollars an hour and she stood on her feet more hours a day than that to get the money that she got. She cleaned hotel rooms on Saturday and Sunday mornings, and she still had no money on any given day and no family members to help her with her only child.

Just knowing her son had no one to help support him became her strength to push ahead to get strong, but at times, pushing did not seem to help. Tara pulled herself forward in spite of the pain and in spite of the fact that she had no outside help. Then, she felt sorry for herself, and she lost the progress that she had made.

Claudetta did her best to talk to her teachers and Rex-Tar's teachers about their school work. She walked to Mrs. Arnold's classroom and stood at her desk until Mrs. Arnold asked to help her. Claudetta took a deep breath before she admitted, "I don't understand the assignment you gave us."

Silence ruled them both for a moment. Claudetta's eyes danced across Mrs. Arnold's desk before Mrs. Arnold said, "Okaaay," in a calming voice. "What don't you understand, Claudetta?" she asked.

"I don't understand any of it. I know what you say you want, but I don't know how to start any of it," Claudetta said.

Mrs. Arnold sat up straight, improving her posture, while she put the palms of her hands down on the desk. "Pull up a chair, Claudetta. Show me what piece you would like to review?"

Claudetta took out a stack of wrinkled, folded papers from her backpack, and she pulled two pages from the top of the stack and pressed them down on the table in the space between herself and Mrs. Arnold.

"Here," Claudetta said. "I don't understand what to do."

"What does this paragraph say?" Mrs. Arnold asked as she pointed to the first paragraph on Claudetta's paper.

After a moment of silence, Claudetta began to call words with no rhythm or change in her speech. Mrs. Arnold leaned over the pages to see the words, all the while she listened for a pause in Claudetta's reading as Claudetta struggled to pronounce every other word on the sheet. Mrs. Arnold looked at the paper and looked back at Claudetta as though she were seeing her for the first time. Claudetta put her fingers on every word she read, even those words she skipped while she read. Mrs. Arnold did not say a word, even when Claudetta did not correctly pronounce many of the words.

Claudetta finished reading the paper, but she whispered, "I still don't understand. That's why I have not finished it. I don't know what I am supposed to be writing."

Mrs. Arnold took the paper and read aloud to Claudetta. When she finished reading, she said, "I need to test your reading so you and I can both know your reading level. Don't worry about finishing the assignment. Bring it to class, and we will look at it as a whole class lesson today," Mrs. Arnold said.

CHAPTER 8

Every day after school, Claudetta took the bus to Rex-Tar's house. These days she not only collected Rex-Tar's schoolwork from his teachers, she turned in his finished work on the days he could not come to school. Today, her mission was to help Mrs. Tara, Rex-Tar's mother, around the house and with dinner. Even Mrs. "Many Questions," her own mother, was not able to object to that anymore. In fact, Mazola had volunteered to help Tara more than once, even offered to drive Tara to the doctor's office for her appointments as she neared the time for her surgery.

Once the secretary, Ms. Garcia, had involved Mazola Rawlings with the news that Claudetta had left school without permission over a week ago, Mazola turned up her presence in Claudetta's life. She put too many questions to Claudetta without stopping until Claudetta burst into tears saying Rex-Tar's mother was sick enough to die. "I'm not doing anything bad," Claudetta had cried. "You check up on me like I killed somebody. I'm helping him with his mother."

Mazola stepped toward her daughter and put her arms around her. "Claudie, Claudie...I didn't know. Believe me. I didn't know."

Claudetta had continued to cry. "I'm lost at school without Rex, Mother. I'm lost without him, and I'm losing him to work. He is always at that restaurant, and when I'm working there, we only get to say, 'Hi', and keep working. And then, there's his mother, who he cannot take care of and work, too. That's why I go there after school, just to help his mother."

"Shhhh," Mazola had whispered. "You have me, Claudie. You have me. We will take care of Rex's mother together. You keep up with your studies, and I will take care of her. Let me take you there so you can introduce me."

CHAPTER 9

Rex-Tar and Claudetta stood outside Mrs. Arnold's English classroom door and waited for her to come to her class. One good thing about attending a specialty high school was the limited number of students who could attend such a school. Jimmy Jurrell High could only have 175 students enrolled at a time.

Both Claudetta and Rex-Tar had spent their ninth and tenth grade years with their zoned or neighborhood high schools where their student count was over 2500 students every semester. Those schools had as many as six assistant principals where their main duty was to clear the halls of students all day long.

Claudetta's face beamed with a smile covering the lower half of her face from simply standing with Rex-Tar. She kept rubbing his arm and hand as she laid her head on his shoulder, only to lift her head off and then rest her head on his shoulder again. Their private reunion was short-lived as their class mates passed by and shook hands with Rex-Tar and welcomed him back to school. Even the girls stopped and said, "Welcome back, Rex."

Claudetta had not told anyone why Rex-Tar was absent when they asked. Only the principal and the attendance clerk-secretary knew Rex was needed to care for and to support his mother for a while. The registrar for the school put many of Rex-Tar's classes online and lifted most of his attendance pressures in the classroom. Still, he had a project with Mrs. Arnold that he needed to turn in to her personally.

Mrs. Arnold started waving her key at them before she reached her door. She fawned over Rex-Tar and smiled all the time she tried to work the key in the door. She invited them inside the classroom, but Claudetta never moved from her position beside the door. "Meet with Rex, first, Mrs. Arnold," Claudetta said.

Claudetta rested her back to the wall as soon as they closed the door. It had been a few days since Mrs. Arnold had leveled her reading only to "kill her dead" by telling her that her reading level was Second-Red. Claudette had whispered the level back to Mrs. Arnold when she heard it, because she couldn't believe it. She had hoped for a color she knew some of her friends had, like purple and bronze or even orange would have been good. Marisol was orange. "Second-Red," she whispered again. "How am I a Second-Red?" she asked. "I'm not that bad, am I?"

Mrs. Arnold had gone through a long speech explaining how no color level was bad. She went on to say that finding out a student's reading level was a good thing, no matter the color. "Now, we know where to start with you," Mrs. Arnold said. "You will see, Claudetta, how much easier your assignments will be for you."

"Second grade level, Mrs. Arnold?" Claudetta asked. "How am I supposed to be happy about reading on a second grade level and I'm a senior in high school?"

"You are looking at this the wrong way, Claudetta. Let's start at the beginning with this. Take one of these books, your choice which one, and come back to me in a few days, and we will start from there."

Claudetta had taken the skinny book and hid it deep inside her purse. With tears in her eyes, she had run out of Mrs. Arnold's class.

Now, standing outside Mrs. Arnold's classroom and every time she saw Mrs. Arnold anywhere, she thought of that horrible meeting with her. She was still asking herself who, among her friends, could she share her pain? *No one,* she thought. *No one.*

"You can come in," Mrs. Arnold said. She had opened the door and stood there a moment waiting for Claudetta to enter. "Claudetta, you can come in now," Mrs. Arnold said, again.

Claudette picked up her back pack from the floor and walked into the classroom. Rex-Tar was still sitting, and he smiled at her as she neared him.

"Uh, no, Mrs. Arnold, I need to see you alone," Claudetta said.

After seeing the look of surprise on Rex-Tar's face and the smile on Mrs. Arnold's face fade, Claudetta added, "It's a girl problem, Rex. Can you give me a few minutes with Mrs. Arnold, please?"

"Oh!," Rex-Tar said, his face suddenly flushed. "I, uh, I will check in with Mr. Woodson about math. Be back in a few."

Claudetta fixed her eyes on Mrs. Arnold and watched her every movement. She kept her tight-lipped position until Rex left the room, and then, Mrs. Arnold spoke first. "I would never discuss your grades or personal information with another student, Claudetta. I thought since you had been the one to pick up Rex-Tar's work that the two of you wanted to talk to me about that."

"No, Ma' am," Claudetta said. "Mrs. Arnold, I'm having a hard time coming to terms with the fact that I read on a second grade level. Rex is my boyfriend, maybe even my future, but I can't tell him that. I want to change that. I want to talk to you about improving my reading. I can't go to college reading on a second grade level."

"As I told you, Claudetta, it's not a permanent reading level. You can work hard and move up the levels."

"I'm ready. What can I do? I can't be at this level. I don't want anyone to know...not my mother, not Rex, and not even Marisol. Rex reads on a black level, and I never see him read anything. Why am I the only one at the stupid level?"

Shaking her head, no, Mrs. Arnold said, "You are not stupid, Claudetta, and neither is your second grade level. A lot of things are important when it comes to reading. Vocabulary plays a large role and reading on a regular, consistent basis. Sit down. You and I are going to set up a plan to get you moving up one level, maybe, within the next six weeks or less. If you are willing, we

can do this," Mrs. Arnold said.

"I'm willing," Claudetta said.

CHAPTER 10

Rex-Tar, Claudetta, and her mother sat in the surgical waiting room of Doctors Without Walls Hospital waiting for a doctor or a nurse or someone to come and talk to Rex-Tar about his mother. Claudetta tried to comfort him, but he could not stay in a seat. He stood at the window and looked out over the City of Houston from the eighth floor of the hospital.

Mrs. Rawlings sat as support for her daughter, Claudetta. More than three hours had passed, and they were still waiting for news. "Fruit, you two?" she asked Rex and Claudetta? Both shook their heads, no, and said, "Not hungry," without even turning around from the window.

The surgery was not supposed to be life-threatening, but the doctor had said that "every time one under goes a surgical procedure, some risks are always there." The ulcers Tara suffered from had been bleeding for a while causing her several areas of pain. The ulcers would make Tara bend over in pain, especially late at night, and early morning on an empty stomach.

Since Rex-Tar worked at night, many nights Tara skipped dinner but had a drink or two or three instead of eating. Between not eating and drinking alcohol, Tara had created a situation that caused her much pain, many tears, and now, a life-changing operation.

Rex-Tar fought with himself standing next to Claudetta, but he was still very much alone. He had stretched his brain to its limits in trying to figure out why his mother had gotten ulcers suddenly? Without any warning signs that Rex could see or know, he asked himself, "why and why now? After weeks of his trying to figure it out without any concrete information, it was Mrs. Rawlings, who took him aside and had "the talk" with him where she hinted at the truth without actually telling him the truth.

All of the strength that Rex-Tar thought his mother had in dealing with the loss of his father and the presence of an illness was just that, a thought. His mother had remained silent through it all. The moments she spent alone were the ones that took her to a place where she didn't have the strength to stand or to ask for help. Instead, she had cooked the lining of her stomach with gin and vodka, during the hours most mothers cooked dinner and put their children to bed. Tara's way of preparing for bed was to get drunk and pass out on her pillows until another sunrise came into view.

Mazola Rawlings, Mrs. Many Questions herself, spent two evenings with Tara alone and discovered more about Tara Dunbar than Rex-Tar had learned about his mother in seventeen years.

Tara worked, and she drank, and she dropped herself into bed to sleep, then she repeated her day. No matter how hard she tried to stop worrying, to stop the loneliness of her life, she worked and she drank, every day. It was not that work was too much for her. It was the "free" time that she had on her hands when she was not working that left her in tears. She hated to go home. Every evening was the time of day when her memories

began. Her fears ballooned, and her concerns for her son left her

feeling helpless. What could she give her only child when all that

she worked did not earn enough? Now, the son who loved her

stood inside a hospital hoping for his mother's life so he could

hold her once again.

CHAPTER 11

Claudetta stood and walked and sat and stood until she could no longer do either. She had given as much of her time as she could this day and her promises to herself and to Mrs. Arnold were never too far from her mind. While everyone else sat and pressed their hands together, Claudetta pulled her tiny book from her purse. It was wrapped with a brown paper bag with no visible evidence of the book title or the reading level of the book. She had wondered a day ago on how she would be able to read her book in public without others being able to read the title or see the Second Red label on the bottom part of the book's spine.

The truth was one simple peek at the book was enough for anyone to see that the book was for a low-level reader. Her only choice had been to buy a package of brown paper bags and cover up every book she had borrowed from Mrs. Arnold's classroom. Her morning saying was, "White level, white level, white level, here I come."

Rex walked over to Claudetta and took a seat. "Maybe, they forgot about me out here," he said.

"Maybe they didn't start on time," Claudetta offered.

"Maybe so," he said. He leaned across Claudetta and asked Mrs. Rawlings, "What do you think?"

"What?" she asked.

"Do you think I should have the lady at the desk check on my mother?"

"It wouldn't hurt," Mrs. Rawlings said.

While Rex-Tar was deciding on whether to question the clerk, the double doors opened and Dr. Cooper, the surgeon, came out, still wearing his surgical cap. He didn't have to call Tara's family, because Rex-Tar was on his feet from the first sight of the doctor. Dr. Cooper motioned for Rex-Tar to follow him to a corner of the waiting room.

"Everything went well," the doctor said. "There was more bleeding than the first test showed, but we have the ulcers under control now."

"When can she go home?" Rex-Tar asked.

"In a few days," the doctor said. "We want to start her on a liquid diet tomorrow and see how well she can keep it down. Then, we will start her on a soft diet and take it from there."

"Doctor," Rex-Tar said in a shaky voice. "Can this condition come back? I mean, what caused my mother to have bleeding inside her stomach? Is it her job?"

For a moment, Dr. Cooper paused, put his hand on Rex-Tar's shoulder and walked him closer to the window by the elevators before he spoke. "Son, what we did was a repair to your mother's bleeding ulcer. That will work as long as your mother stops drinking. Contrary to some beliefs, bleeding ulcers are not brought on by just a domestic job."

"Drinking?" Rex asked.

"I'm sorry, Son."

"When can I see her?" Rex-Tar asked.

"Your mother is being cleaned up in the O.R., and is about to be sent to the recovery room. In about an hour, a nurse will come and get you and take you to see her."

"Thank you, Dr. Cooper," Rex-Tar said, then, put his hand out to the doctor.

Rex-Tar eased his way back to his seat beside Claudetta and laid back in the chair, resting the back of his head on the back of the seat. Both Claudetta and her mother looked at him, then, at each other.

"She's going to be okay, Rex," Claudetta said. She got on her knees in her chair and leaned over him, trying to see his face. Even with tears leaking out the corners of his eyes, he kept them closed.

"I'm glad the doctor told you," Mrs. Rawlings said. "She

will need your support now that you know."

CHAPTER 12

Crying was the first thing that Rex-Tar had to over-come. If he were going to be of any good to his mother, he had to be over his emotions. He sat in the waiting room's restroom as long as he could with random people knocking on the door to use it. He allowed himself a little time to mend. It seemed that he had to mature five years in five minutes. If people were not looking at him, they were depending on him. Either way, he had to put off his feelings for a time.

He tried to send Claudetta home with her mother while he waited in the hospital to see his own mother, but Claudetta refused to leave him. In the two years that they had gone out, he had never cried in front of her. It was he who had tried to be strong for her and for his mother. Now, without his even asking for anything, Claudetta had taken the role of stroking him. Instead of it making him stronger, it made him want to cry in her arms. And that could not be.

Without opening her eyes, Tara Dunbar could hear her son's pain in the way he said, "Mother." Even though the effects of her medications were wearing off, she kept her eyes closed while her son cried his pain over her still body. Hearing him say her name told her that somehow, he knew about her drinking. No matter how much she heard him sob, she knew she could not bear to see the pain in his eyes. His broken voice haunted her even after he left the recovery room. Tara's eyes leaked tears and even she did not know if they were from her wounds that hurt from surgery or from the pain in her heart.

CHAPTER 13

"You have to let her tell you, Rex," Claudetta said. "Your mother loves you, but you have to open up and let her inside you. She needs to tell you about her drinking."

"She could have told me. Don't make this my fault that she didn't tell me," he said.

Claudetta walked into his arms and held him around his neck. "You have a way of making people too afraid, too ashamed to tell you their weaknesses, whether you intend to or know it or not."

He stiffened his body and tried to pull away, but she continued to hold him and talk to him until he relaxed. "People want to be strong for you, Rex, even when they cannot."

His silence abled her to continue talking. "I cannot read well, Rex. I mean, I read poorly, worse than you, worse than Marisol, and worse than anybody I know at the school. I really suck at reading, and I hid it from you. I hid it from my mom. I hid it from Marisol."

"So you blame me for that, too?" he asked. "I mean, do you blame me because you kept a secret from me?"

"No. I blame me that I feel like a loser, a failure, telling you, my boyfriend, that I read on a second grade level. I'm sure your mom probably blames herself that you now know that she has a drinking problem and that she made herself sick because of it. None of us is perfect, Rex."

"I know that, Claudie. I never expect anyone to be perfect. I'm not perfect. I try hard every day just to get by. There are times that I don't think I'm going to graduate. I try hard for my mom and for you. I don't have a dad or an uncle or a grandfather. I have nobody male to go to in my life but a few teachers who have a few minutes to spare. I'm supposed to be a man, but how can I be?"

"We can 'be' anything and everything as long as we are together. You are not alone, Rex. I am not alone either. We have each other, and we have our moms. We can get pass this. We have to open up to each other and help each other. I love you."

"I love you, too, Claudie," Rex said. He pulled her tighter and rested his face on her head. "Is it okay to be afraid, sometimes?" he asked.

"Yes, it is, as long as we share our fears and don't hide them from each other. It's okay. Life is hard and scary for a lot of people, not just for us. Some people pretend everything is great. The truth is life is more than it seems."

"Life is scary, Claudie, and I'm a man."

"Being a man is not about being alone, Rex. We are partners."

"We will see. Let's go and get my mother from the hospital, together; you and I can help her to get through this, as a family, as partners. "